I Will Not Lose in SUPER SHOES!

For my three speedy speedsters!—JF

PENGUIN WORKSHOP
An imprint of Penguin Random House LLC, New York

First published simultaneously in paperback and hardcover in the United States of America
by Penguin Workshop, an imprint of Penguin Random House LLC, New York, 2022

Visit us online at penguinrandomhouse.com.

Library of Congress Cataloging-in-Publication Data is available.

Manufactured in China

ISBN 9780593384534 (pbk)   10 9 8 7 6 5 4 3 2 1 TOPL

I Will Not Lose in SUPER SHOES!

by Jonathan Fenske

Penguin Workshop

I am
BOOK-IT BUNNY,
see?

Who can read
as fast as
ME?

4

I **RACE** through
books on speedy feet!
I almost never can be beat!

And with my brand-new Super Shoes there is **NO WAY** that I can lose!

So turn the page,
pick up the pace,
and join me in a
READING RACE!

Here I go!
I hit my stride.

LOOK DOWN!

Why are your shoes untied?

I see you want
to race **FOR REAL!**

Watch out
for the
banana peel!

SPROING!

SPLAT!

Hmmm.
I see
you did
not slip.

STOP!
Do I hear something SCARY?
Something CREEPY?
Something HAIRY?

I am brave.
I have no fear.
My sneaky shoes
will get me near.

I will go.

You wait
RIGHT HERE!

MEOW

Silly me!
Imagine that!

The scary thing
is just a
CAT!

Oh no!
THE END
is coming fast!

I need some
SUPER TURBO BLAST!

RUMBLE!

RUMBLE!

T

THE END

You won. So what?
I thought you might.
(My Super Shoes
were kind of tight.)

TODAY was
just a racing test.
Yippee. You passed.
Go get some rest.

TOMORROW I will
try my best.

31

Oh. By the way, could someone use some almost brand-new SUPER SHOES?